# Inside the NBA

# New Jersey Nets

**Paul Joseph**

**ABDO & Daughters**
P U B L I S H I N G

Published by Abdo & Daughters, 4940 Viking Dr., Suite 622, Edina, MN 55435.

Cover photo: Duomo
Interior photos: Allsport, pages 1, 26, 28
                   Wide World Photos, pages 5, 9, 11, 13, 15, 21, 23, 24, 25

**Edited by Kal Gronvall**


**Library of Congress Cataloging–in–Publication Data**

Joseph, Paul, 1970-
   The New Jersey Nets / by Paul Joseph
      p.  cm. — (Inside the NBA)
   Includes index.
   Summary: Provides an overview of the history and key personalities connected with the team that started out as the New Jersey Americans in the American Basketball Association (ABA) in 1967.
   ISBN  1-56239-766-4
   1. New Jersey Nets (Basketball team)—Juvenile literature.
[1. New Jersey Nets (Basketball team)—History. 2. Basketball—History.]  I. Title. II. Series.
GV885.52.N37J67  1997
796.323' 64' 09749—dc21                  96-39615
                                           CIP
                                           AC

# Contents

# New Jersey Nets

The New Jersey Nets franchise has had a long and frustrating ride through the National Basketball Association (NBA). The Nets were born in 1967. They were known at the time as the New Jersey Americans in the brand-new league, the American Basketball Association (ABA). The Nets were always overshadowed by their cross-town rival, the New York Knicks.

The Nets had a problem filling the seats. Then they made a trade for the greatest player in ABA history and one of the greatest in NBA history, Julius "Dr. J" Erving. Dr. J came to the Nets and was an instant sensation. The Nets began winning and filling the stands.

Erving led the Nets to two ABA titles, he grabbed three Most Valuable Player Awards (MVP), and was the player to watch in either league. Then the NBA and ABA merged in 1976 and Dr. J was lured to the Philadelphia 76ers with a big-money deal.

The merger of the ABA with the NBA hit the Nets hard. They had already lost Dr. J, their star player, and they had to pay a huge fee to join the NBA. Even worse, they could not draft any players in the college draft that year.

*Facing page:* The Nets' Jayson Williams leaps in the air to keep the ball inbounds.

From 1976 to the present, the Nets have enjoyed little success. They have made the playoffs about half the seasons in the NBA, only to lose in the first round every time but once. It even took them four tries in the playoffs to get their first win.

For the Nets, the frustration continues. They have gone through many owners, many coaches, different team names, great players, horrible players, different arenas, and even different leagues.

Today the Nets look to new head coach John Calipari, rebounding sensation Jayson Williams, big-time scorer Jim Jackson, All-Star Chris Gatling, and future star Kerry Kittles to lead the franchise to championship form. The franchise has tasted success in the ABA, but now they want to taste it in the NBA.

# Joining The ABA

The New Jersey Americans made their ABA debut on October 23, 1967. The team averaged just 2,000 in attendance and lost money. On the bright side New Jersey guard Lavern Tart led the team in scoring with a 23-point-per-game average, which was third in the entire ABA. He also set a single-game scoring record with 49 points.

In 1967, New Jersey finished their first season with 36 wins—tied for the last playoff spot with Kentucky. In a one-game playoff between the two teams, New Jersey received the home-court advantage. The game was originally scheduled for the Teaneck Armory, New Jersey's home court. But a circus was already scheduled for the building on that day. As a result, the game was moved to the Commack Arena in New York. However, when the two teams arrived, the floor was unplayable—pieces of wood were sticking out, and there were loose bolts and nuts everywhere. With no other place in which to play, New Jersey had to forfeit its first playoff game.

In 1968, two changes took place. The New Jersey Americans became the New York Nets, and the team moved to Commack Arena.

The floor was fixed for the Nets, but the team wasn't. The Nets won only 17 games—the fewest wins in ABA history.

The horrible 1968 season was capped off by the lowest attendance mark in team history. The Nets averaged about 1,000 fans per game. New Jersey was a hard sell because the Knicks and a better league were playing across town.

In 1969, the Nets thought that their luck was turning around when Lew Alcindor (later Kareem Abdul-Jabbar) said he would like to play in New York. The three-time College Player of the Year was wanted by every team in the NBA too. The ABA draft rights were awarded to the Nets so that Alcindor, a New York City native, could play close to home and finally help turn the Nets around. In the NBA, the Milwaukee Bucks had the rights to him.

Alcindor told both teams he would accept one sealed bid from each team, the team with the highest bid would get the rights to him. Because Alcindor would boost the league's attendance, all of the ABA teams agreed to help pay the cost of his huge contract. But the Nets' owner, Arthur Brown, submitted a lower bid, intending to raise it when needed. True to his word, Alcindor took the Bucks' better offer, and the Nets did not get a second chance. One of the greatest players in basketball history had just slipped through the Nets' hands.

Nets' star Lavern Tart in action.

# The Nets Get A New Owner

After losing out on Lew Alcindor, Brown sold his team to Roy Boe in 1969. Boe moved the Nets to the Island Garden in Long Island, New York. Boe also was pushing for a new arena for his team.

The Nets surprised everyone and won 39 games and a spot in the playoffs. Tart led the team again with a 24-point scoring average. Newly acquired Lloyd Dove chipped in 14 points and 7 rebounds per game. In the playoffs the Nets lost to Kentucky in a back-and-forth, seven-game battle.

Besides the playoff surprise, the Nets jumped in attendance to 4,000 per game. And New York fan-favorite Lou (Looie) Carnesecca left New York's St. John's University and took over as the new coach of the Nets.

The team was excited about their chances in 1970. The team was young, well coached, and a new star had just joined the team. Boe acquired Rick Barry from Virginia. Barry immediately made an impact on the Nets. He was second in the league in scoring with 29 points per game, led the league in free-throw shooting with 89 percent, and was the first Net named to the All-ABA Team.

# Barry Leads The Nets

The Nets won a franchise-best 40 games and were headed to the playoffs. But in the playoffs Barry couldn't carry the team. The Nets lost in the first round in six games.

In the 1971-72 season it looked as though the foundation had been laid for both the ABA, which was in its fifth year, and the Nets, which were led by Carnesecca and Barry, both now in their second year.

Rick Barry was second again in scoring, this time averaging 31 points, and repeated as free-throw champ. Carnesecca had great talent surrounding Barry and knew how to use them. The team jumped past .500 for the first time with a 44-40 record.

In the playoffs the Nets gave it everything they had. They ousted the Kentucky Colonels—the best team in the league—in the first round. Against the Virginia Squires they surprised everyone and took the series in seven hard-fought games.

The surprising Nets had made it to the ABA Championship. In the championship the Nets played the Indiana Pacers tough for six games until the Pacers finally pulled it off.

The Nets had built a championship caliber team with great fan support. Attendance averaged more than 12,000 per game in the playoffs and two games with Indiana drew 15,000 each.

But then it all came crashing down. Rick Barry was ordered by a judge to return to the NBA. The Nets were not the same. They did acquire 6-foot, 11-inch center Jim Chones and point guard Brian Taylor who both made the All-Rookie team.

Chones and Taylor led the Nets to the playoffs, only to lose in the first round to the Carolina Cougars. Cougars head coach Larry Brown summed up the season for the Nets: "Sometimes the Nets players stand around like they are waiting for Rick Barry to come back."

The Nets' players and fans did hope that Barry would come back. But that never happened. Somebody even better showed up—a doctor, who gave the team the medicine it needed: a championship.

Rick Barry lays one in for an easy two against the Kentucky Colonels.

# The Doctor Has The Cure

The 1973-74 season saw the Nets lose a great coach and saw the arrival of the greatest player in franchise history. Coach Carnesecca had missed college ball and returned to St. Johns. And Julius Erving was purchased from the Virginia Squires.

Erving was known as "Dr. J" because of the surgical precision with which he dismantled his opponents. He was everything a great basketball player should be. Dr. J could pass, shoot, play defense, and hang in the air unlike any other player before him. Dr. J was the new star that kids all across the country tried to play like—including a young boy in North Carolina named Michael Jordan.

Erving was admired just as much for his leadership as he was for his playing ability. He got the team going in the locker-room when they needed a boost. He worked hard and played hard, and everyone looked up to him.

In his first year with the Nets, Erving was the ABA scoring champ with a 27-points-per-game average. He was also third in steals, fourth in assists, and won the MVP Award.

Behind the Doc, the Nets finished the season with an incredible 55 wins, the ABA's best. They dumped Virginia and Kentucky in the first two rounds and were headed to the Championship.

Against the Utah Stars the Nets again dominated, winning the ABA Championship in five games. Erving was named Finals MVP and the Nets had their first-ever title.

Julius "Dr. J" Erving (32) and teammate Brian Taylor (35) struggle for a rebound.

# Another Championship

The Nets made few changes for the 1974-75 season. After a championship season, with the most wins of any other team in the league, the highest average attendance, and Dr. J, there wasn't much more the team could do.

Erving again was named the league's MVP as he led the Nets to an even more impressive 58 wins. But in the playoffs, the Nets were shocked in five quick games by St. Louis, a team they had gone 12-0 against in the regular season.

The following year, Doc was determined to avenge the playoff disaster of the previous season. Erving dominated the league, winning the scoring title with a 29-point scoring average. He was again the regular season MVP as the Nets won 55 games.

In the All-Star Game that year, Erving became legendary. In the first-ever Slam-Dunk contest, Erving took off from the foul line and soared to the hoop—something basketball fans had never seen before. He not only won the Slam-Dunk contest, he was named the All-Star Game's MVP.

In the playoffs, Erving single-handedly took the Nets all the way. Against Denver in the ABA Championship, Erving made game-winning shots, led his team back to victory after being down by 22, and scored 45 points in one game. Again Dr. J and the Nets were ABA Champions—in fact, the last ABA Champions.

Dr. J and his teammates celebrate after the Nets' victory over the Denver Nuggets in the 1976 ABA Championship Series.

# Hello NBA, Farewell Dr. J

In 1976, the ABA folded. It didn't mean the end for the Nets, though. On June 17, the Nets were accepted into the NBA along with three other teams from the ABA: the Denver Nuggets, Indiana Pacers, and San Antonio Spurs.

The price for joining the NBA was steep for these teams. Each team had to pay $3.2 million to the NBA, and the Nets had to pay an additional $480,000 penalty per year for 10 years to the New York Knicks for infringing on their territory.

The Nets were strapped for cash, so Boe offered Dr. J to the Knicks in exchange for not having to pay the infringement fee. The Knicks refused. Then the Philadelphia 76ers offered Boe $3 million in cash for Erving, and Boe accepted.

The greatest player in Nets' history was gone. Many wondered if the Doc could continue his magic in the NBA. He proved that he could. He picked up the league's MVP Award and led his Sixers to an NBA title.

Julius Erving retired in 1987 as the third-highest scorer in pro basketball history, with 30,026 points. During his three-year stay with the Nets the team went 168-84, having its only 50-plus win seasons. In addition, the team was 21-11 in the playoffs. But now the "Erving Era" was over.

The Nets were in the NBA, but the team was in shambles. For the first three seasons, they could not share in television revenue and could not take part in the 1976 college draft.

When their first season in the NBA started, the Nets had a very weak line-up. Their one bright spot was the trade they had made to acquire Nate "Tiny" Archibald, the only player ever to win scoring and assists titles in the same season. Tiny was having a great season for the Nets, averaging 20 points per game, until breaking his ankle in the 34th game. That injury finished his season.

The Nets finished their inaugural season in the NBA with a 22-60 record—worst in all of basketball.

# Back To New Jersey

For their second season in the NBA, the Nets decided to move back to New Jersey and were renamed the New Jersey Nets. The Nets, however, did get a draft pick that year and used it on Bernard King.

After trading Tiny Archibald, King was now considered the go-to guy. King was a sensation for the Nets, averaging 24 points per game and nearly 10 rebounds. But even with this new star the Nets could only produce two more wins from the previous season, finishing 24-58, again the NBA's worst record.

For the 1978-79 season the Nets had new ownership. Joseph Taub and Alan Cohen purchased the Nets franchise from Boe, who was financially drained by the Nets and the NBA.

On the court, the Nets improved by 13 wins and made the NBA playoffs for the first time. King and John Williamson led the way for the Nets, each scoring 22 points per game. Although the Nets were swept in the playoffs by Dr. J and the 76ers, it was still a very successful season for the up-and-coming Nets.

In the next two seasons the Nets went backwards and fell short of making the playoffs. In 1979-80, they won 34 games, and in 1980-81, they fell to 24 wins. The Nets made trades and tried different line-ups. In a surprising move, they sent their best player, Bernard King, to the Utah Jazz.

If the Nets wanted to get better and compete in the NBA, they knew they had to make changes and get new players. The biggest move was acquiring a new coach.

17

# New Jersey

Nets' guard Lavern Tart led the team in scoring during their 1967-68 season debut, averaging 23 points per game.

During his first season with the Nets in 1970-71, Rick Barry was second in the league with 29 points per game, and was the first Net named to the All-ABA Team.

In his debut 1973-74 season with the Nets, Julius "Dr. J" Erving was the ABA scoring champ, with a 27-points-per-game average. He also was third in steals, fourth in assists, and won the MVP Award.

# Nets

Buck Williams earned the NBA's Rookie of the Year Award for the 1981-82 season. He was also the first Net to play in the NBA All-Star Game.

Drazen Petrovic finished the 1992-93 season with an average of 22 points per game, third in three-point percentage, and ninth in free throw shooting, winning him a spot on the All-NBA Third Team.

Guard Kerry Kittles was the Nets' eighth pick in the 1996 NBA Draft. He was named to the 1996-97 All-Rookie Second Team.

# Larry Brown Takes Over

The Nets had a whole new look for the 1981-82 season. Larry Brown took over as coach, and the Nets grabbed Buck Williams in the draft. Williams was an instant sensation, earning the NBA's Rookie of the Year Award. Buck Williams was also the first Net to play in the NBA All-Star Game, which happened to be played at the Nets new home, the Meadowland's Brendan Byrne Arena.

The Nets also drafted Albert King, brother of Bernard, and Ray Tolbert. They acquired Ray Williams and Otis Birdsong in trades. Brown had his young squad ready to compete.

The Nets finished the year 44-38, the team's first winning year in the NBA. The 20-win improvement was the league's best. But in the playoffs the Nets were not only upset but also swept by the Washington Bullets. It was a disappointing end to a great season.

The following season the Nets improved even more. Buck Williams and King were the scoring leaders for the Nets with 17 points a game. Charismatic center Darryl Dawkins came over from the Sixers, and Michael Ray Richardson came from the Golden State Warriors to add some energy and offensive power to the team.

Larry Brown's changes worked, as the Nets won 49 games—their best NBA record in franchise history to date. But the season was marred towards the end. The man most responsible for turning the team around—Larry Brown—had accepted a job with the University of Kansas. Brown was fired with six games remaining and the Nets never recovered. They were again swept in the playoffs by the Knicks.

Buck Williams slams one home.

# The Nets Win A Playoff Game

Stan Albeck took over as coach of the Nets and promised a victory in the playoffs. The 1983-84 season was going as Albeck had planned. Darryl Dawkins had his best NBA season with 16 points and 7 rebounds per game. Buck Williams and Richardson were again playing solid ball, while Birdsong topped the scoring at 20 points per game.

The Nets came on strong at the end of the season, winning 19 of their last 25 games to gain a third straight playoff berth with a 45-37 record.

Now it was on to the playoffs. The Nets were matched against the defending champion 76ers. Many wondered if they could win that one playoff game that Albeck had promised. They not only won a game, they shocked and upset the 76ers by winning the series.

The Nets won two more playoff games in the next series before falling to the Milwaukee Bucks in six. It was the best NBA season for the Nets.

In 1984-85, the Nets had an injury-packed season. They logged an incredible 223 games missed due to injury. The Nets had to use 13 different starting lineups throughout the year. But they did manage to collect 42 wins and a spot in the playoffs. But the injured Nets were bounced by the Detroit Pistons in three straight games.

The following season the Nets ended a string of four straight winning seasons with a 39-43 record. They did, however, make a fifth consecutive playoff appearance. The team was again swept, this time by the Bucks.

It got even worse in 1986 as the Nets continued with injuries and plummeted to a 24-58 record and missed the playoffs.

The Nets then hit rock bottom. For the next three years, the team averaged 20 wins a season, winning only 17 games in 1989-90. Coaching changes, trades, free agents, and draft choices couldn't help the Nets. Then in 1990, they got the number one pick in the NBA draft.

# The Nets Get Coleman

Finally, luck had come the Nets way when they won the 1990 May draft lottery. In June, they selected Syracuse forward Derrick Coleman, who would go on to become 1990-91 Rookie of the Year.

Reggie Theus, who came over from the Orlando Magic, led the team in scoring with 19 points per game. Coleman was right behind him with 18, while finishing in the top 10 in the NBA for rebounds. Second-year head coach Bill Fitch posted his 800th NBA win to highlight the season.

In mid-season, the Nets acquired Terry Mills and Drazen Petrovic through trades. The Nets improved to 26 wins and were looking forward to the following season.

The Nets got the second pick in the NBA Draft in 1991, and chose point guard Kenny Anderson from Georgia Tech. With the addition of Anderson, the team reached the playoffs for the first time since 1986.

Petrovic led the team in scoring with 20 points per game, while Coleman led the team in rebounds with 10. In the playoffs, however, the Nets again couldn't get a win. They were swept by the Cleveland Cavilers in four straight. Bill Fitch had seen enough and resigned.

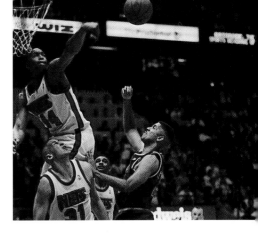

*Right:* Derrick Coleman rejects a shot.

Nets' coach Chuck Daly yells instructions to his team.

# Chuck Daly Gives It A Try

In 1992, Chuck Daly, who guided the Detroit Pistons to two NBA Championships and the United States "Dream Team" to the 1992 Olympic Gold Medal, took over as the head coach of the Nets.

Daly made an immediate impression on his young team. His winning attitude helped build a new Nets team. The team finished the 1992-93 season with 42 wins, and they were breathing down the necks of the first place Knicks.

Kenny Anderson was running the show from the point while Petrovic and Coleman were the offensive machines. Petrovic made the All-NBA Third Team after finishing with 22 points, third in three-point percentage, and ninth in free throw shooting. Coleman chipped in 20 points per game and was in the top 10 in rebounding with 11.

In the playoffs the Nets lost key players to injuries. Anderson was out with a broken wrist, as were Sam Bowie and Chris Dudley. Petrovic and Coleman gave it their all in the playoffs, almost taking Cleveland by themselves. But in the end the Cavilers were too much for the Nets.

Kenny Anderson drives past the Knicks' defense.

In June, the NBA and the international basketball community were shocked and saddened when Petrovic was killed in a car accident in his home country of Germany. His death left the Nets with an enormous hole to fill, both on the court and in their hearts.

The Nets suffered a difficult start to the 1993-94 season. Both emotionally, due to the death of their friend and teammate Petrovic, and physically due to injuries to key players. But Daly got the team re-focused and they started playing better ball.

Kenny Anderson and Derrick Coleman became the first Nets ever elected to start in the NBA All-Star Game. The Nets continued to play well in the second half of the season and finished with 45 wins—their second best record in the NBA.

In the playoffs the Nets were matched against their cross-river rival, the New York Knicks. The Nets had taken four out of five regular season games from the Knicks. But in the playoffs the Nets stumbled, winning only one game and losing the series.

Chuck Daly retired from coaching after the playoffs to pursue a broadcasting career with both the Nets and WTBS.

Drazen Petrovic gets set to pass.

# Rebuilding Again

In 1994-95, the Nets won only 30 games and missed out on the playoffs. Coleman again was the offensive force, scoring 20 points per game.

The following season the team signed, traded, and drafted many players. They had almost all new faces on the team, and the result was an identical 30-52 record and another year out of the playoffs.

On November 30, New Jersey traded star forward Derrick Coleman, Sean Higgins, and Rex Walters to Philadelphia for 7-foot, 6-inch center Shawn Bradley, Tim Perry, and Greg Graham. Then on January 19, point guard Kenny Anderson and Gerald Glass were shipped to the Charlotte Hornets for Kendall Gill and Khalid Reeves.

Ed O'Bannon was the Nets' ninth pick in the draft, and played well for a rookie. Jayson Williams came into his own as both an offensive and defensive rebounding specialist. The following season the rebuilding continued. This time, however, it started with a new head coach.

John Calipari took over as executive vice president and head coach of the Nets in 1996 and continued to rebuild. He was the University of Massachusetts head coach before taking the job with the Nets. He enjoyed huge success coaching UMASS, using tenacious defense and a solid offensive scheme, which he hopes to bring to the Nets.

Calipari's first move for the Nets was picking guard Kerry Kittles with the eighth pick in the 1996 draft. The 6-foot, 5-inch Kittles has tremendous offensive and defensive abilities. After a solid season he was named to the 1996-97 All-Rookie Second Team.

Calipari made another big move in the middle of the 1996-97 season. He was involved in the biggest trade of the season. The Nets sent the NBA's leading shot-blocker, Shawn Bradley, to the Dallas Mavericks for Jim Jackson and All-Star Chris Gatling. The trade also included the Mavericks Sam Cassell, George McCloud, and Eric Montross for the Nets' Khalid Reeves, Robert Pack, and Ed O'Bannon. Most NBA experts believe the Nets got the much better end of the deal.

With tough-talking Calipari leading the Nets from the bench, Jayson Williams pulling down the rebounds, Sam Cassell dishing the assists, Jim Jackson being an offensive threat, Gatling scoring and

rebounding, and the new kid on the block, Kittles doing it all, the Nets are a sure bet to improve. In fact, with a foundation like that, the New Jersey Nets should be back in the playoffs soon, and be vying for their first-ever NBA championship.

Kerry Kittles drives the ball down the court.

# Glossary

**American Basketball Association (ABA)**—A professional basketball league that rivaled the NBA from 1967 to 1976 until it merged with the NBA.

**assist**—A pass of the ball to the teammate scoring a field goal.

**Basketball Association of America (BAA)**—A professional basketball league that merged with the NBL to form the NBA.

**center**—A player who holds the middle position on the court.

**championship**—The final basketball game or series, to determine the best team.

**draft**—An event held where NBA teams choose amateur players to be on their team.

**expansion team**—A newly-formed team that joins an already established league.

**fast break**—A play that develops quickly down court after a defensive rebound.

**field goal**—When a player scores two or three points with one shot.

**Finals**—The championship series of the NBA playoffs.

**forward**—A player who is part of the front line of offense and defense.

**franchise**—A team that belongs to an organized league.

**free throw**—A privilege given a player to score one point by an unhindered throw for goal from within the free-throw circle and behind the free-throw line.

**guard**—Either of two players who initiate plays from the center of the court.

**jump ball**—To put the ball in play in the center restraining circle with a jump between two opponents at the beginning of the game, each extra period, or when two opposing players each have control of the ball.

**Most Valuable Player (MVP) Award**—An award given to the best player in the league, All-Star Game, or NBA Finals.

**National Basketball Association (NBA)**—A professional basketball league in the United States and Canada, consisting of the Eastern and Western conferences.

**National Basketball League (NBL)**—A professional basketball league that merged with the BAA to form the NBA.

**National Collegiate Athletic Association (NCAA)**—The ruling body which oversees all athletic competition at the college level.

**personal foul**—A player foul which involves contact with an opponent while the ball is alive or after the ball is in the possession of a player for a throw-in.

**playoffs**—Games played by the best teams after the regular season to determine a champion.

**postseason**—All the games after the regular season ends; the playoffs.

**rebound**—To grab and control the ball after a missed shot.

**rookie**—A first-year player.

**Rookie of the Year Award**—An award given to the best first-year player in the league.

**Sixth Man Award**—An award given yearly by the NBA to the best non-starting player.

**trade**—To exchange a player or players with another team.

# Index